PAW Patrol

Super Sticker Fun!

W9-BUN-189

A GOLDEN BOOK • NEW YORK

ISBN 978-0-525-57788-1

rhcbooks.com

MANUFACTURED IN CHINA

10 9 8 7 6 5 4

MAKE A PAW PATROL STICKER PUZZLE!

- Choose a puzzle and find the matching sticker page.

- Have a grown-up help you remove the puzzles and sticker pages from this book.

- Match the sticker pieces to the numbered spaces in the puzzle.

PUZZLE 1

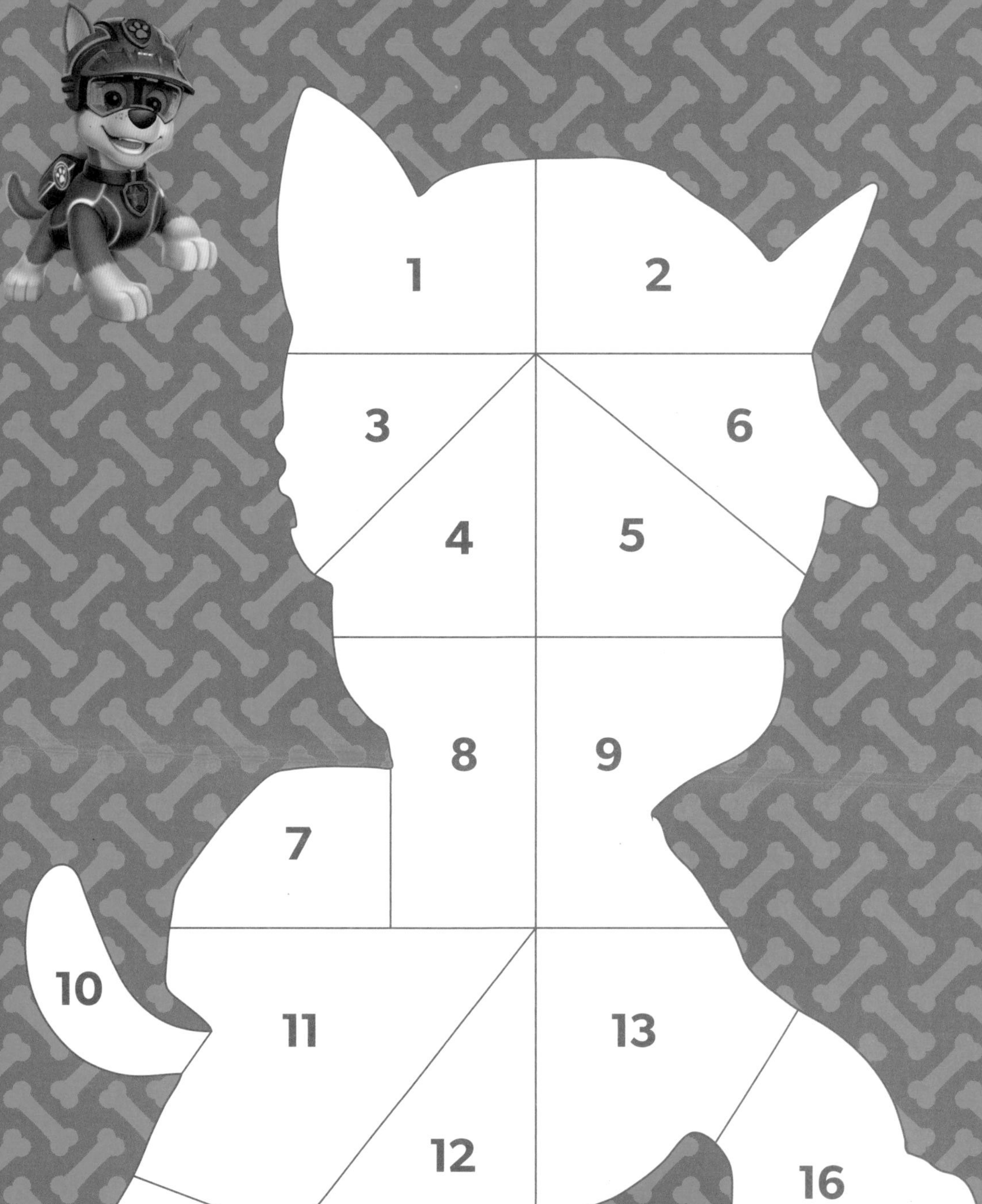

Color the bottom picture of Chase so it matches the top picture.

Circle the Marshall who is different.

A

B

C

D

PUZZLE 2

1   2

3   4   5

6

7   8

9   10

11

12   13   14

Match each member of the team to his or her close-up.

A

B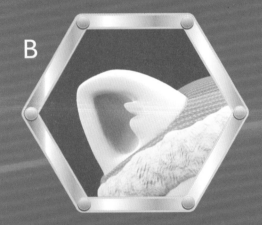

C

1

2

3

Help Rubble get to his Digger.

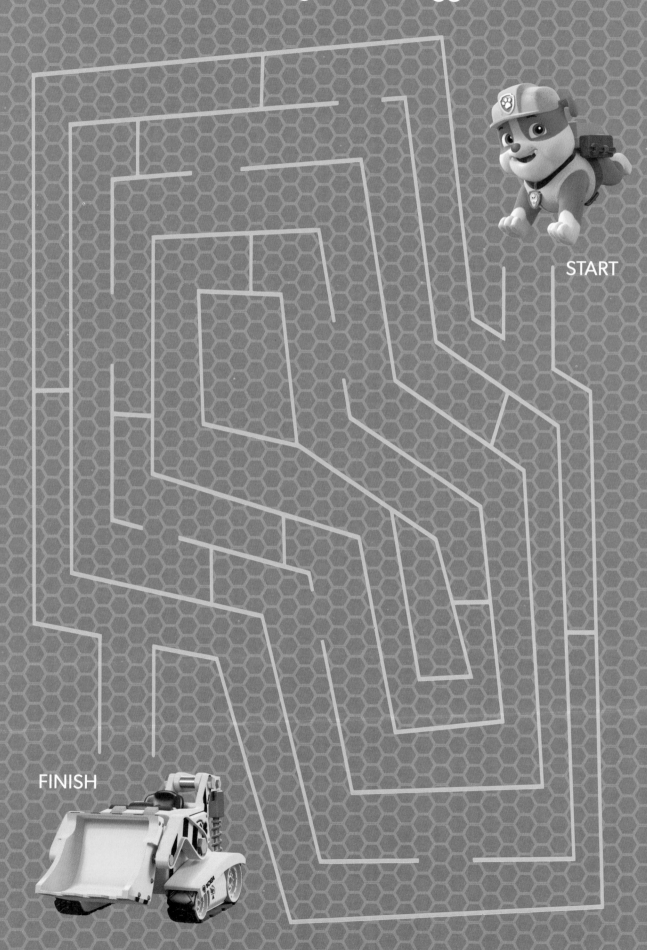

START

FINISH

1

2

3

4

5

6

7

8

9

10

11

12

13

14

15

Draw a helmet for Rubble.

Draw a bright, shiny sun for Skye.

1

2

3

6

4

5

7

9

11

8

10

13

12

14

17

15

16

1

2

3

4

5

6

7

8

9

13

10

12

11

14

15

16

Skye's got to fly!
Help her find Rubble.

START

FINISH

Match each member of the team to his or her vehicle.

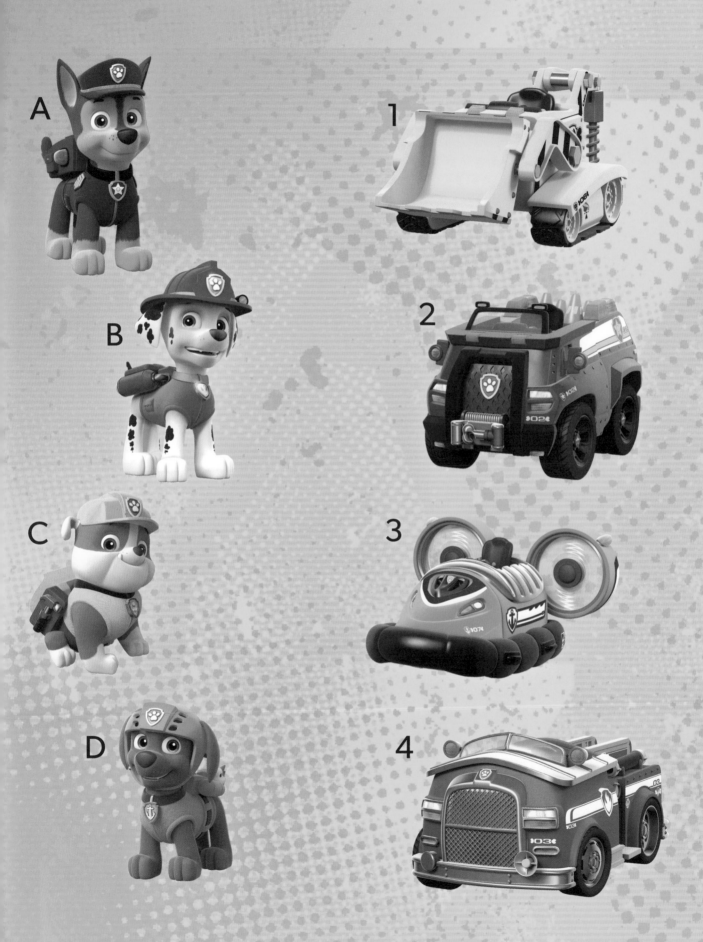

A

B

C

D

1

2

3

4

E

5

F

6

G

7

ANSWER: A-2, B-4, C-1, D-3, E-6, F-5, and G-7.

Draw a fish for Zuma to say hello to.

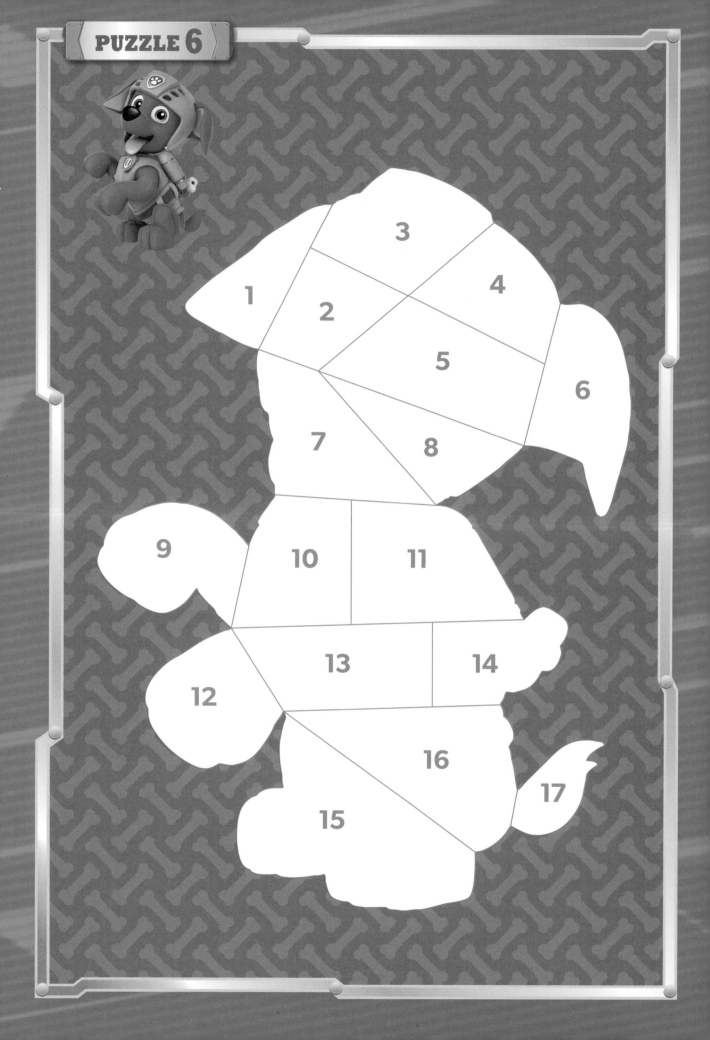

9

15

10

16

4

13

11

2

6

1

14

3

7

12

8

5

10

6

7

1

4

13

2

11

8

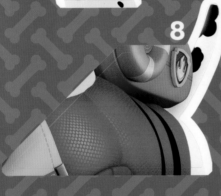

12

5

9

3

14

7

5

8

13

14

9

12

15

2

11

4

3

10

1

6

PUZZLE 4

3

11

12

9

4

13

14

10

6

1

5

2

16

17

8

7

15

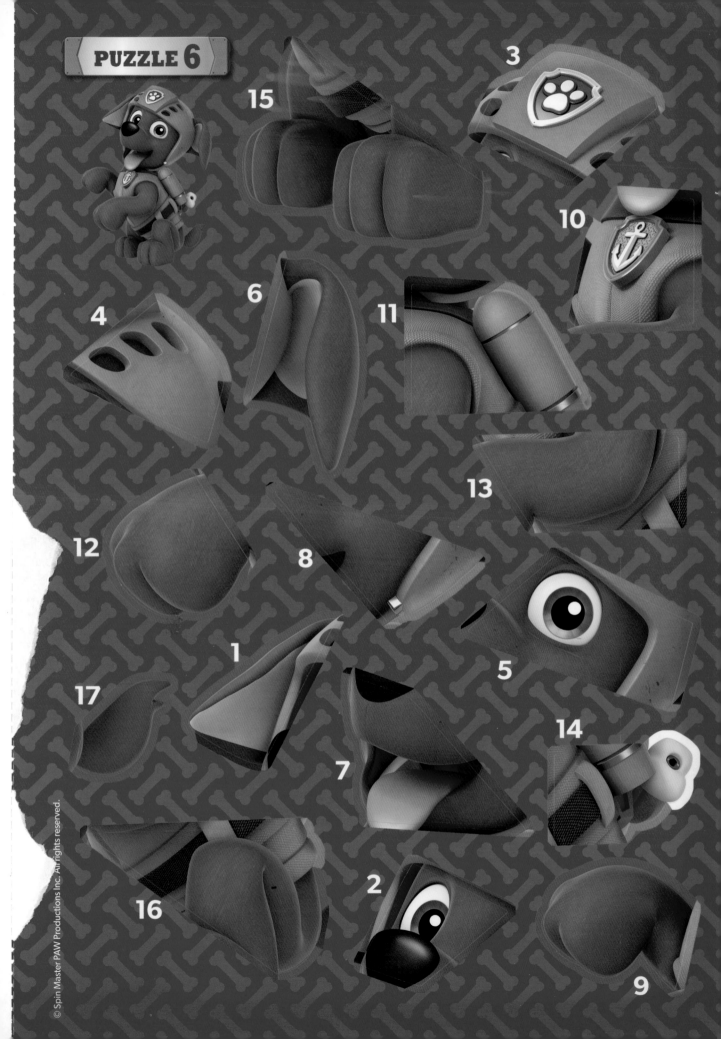

PUZZLE 6

15

3

10

4

6

11

12

8

13

1

17

5

7

14

16

2

9

PUZZLE 7

13

8

1

15

4

7

5

2

9

3

14

12

10

6

11

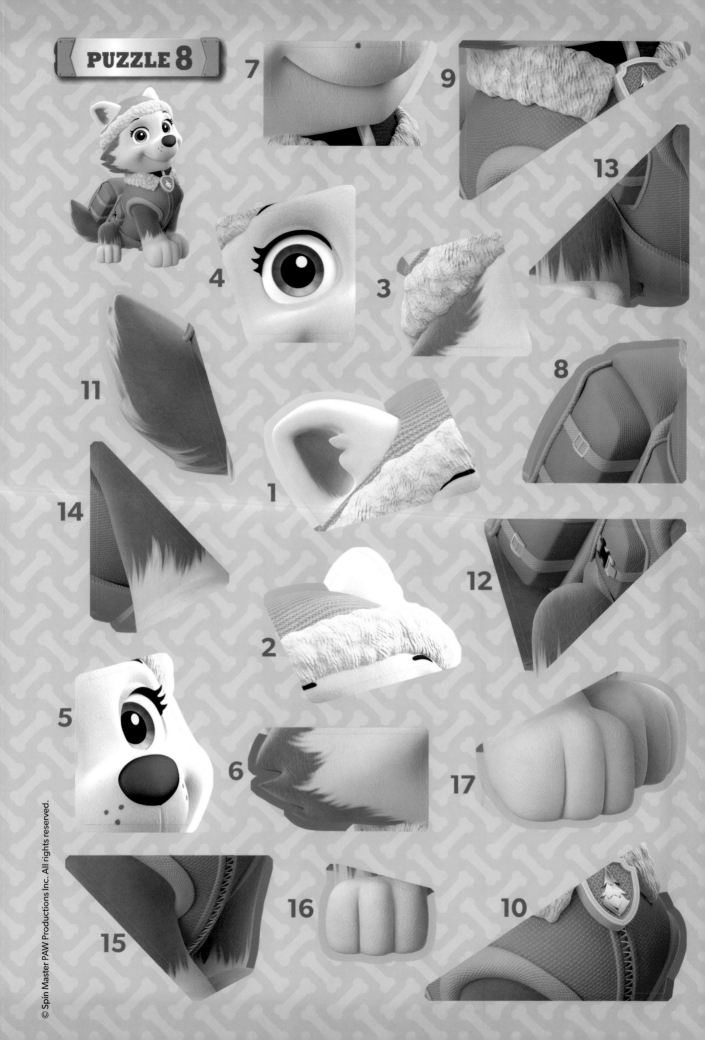

PUZZLE 8

PUZZLE 9

2

12

14

3

15

4

10

9

1

8

13

7

6

11

5

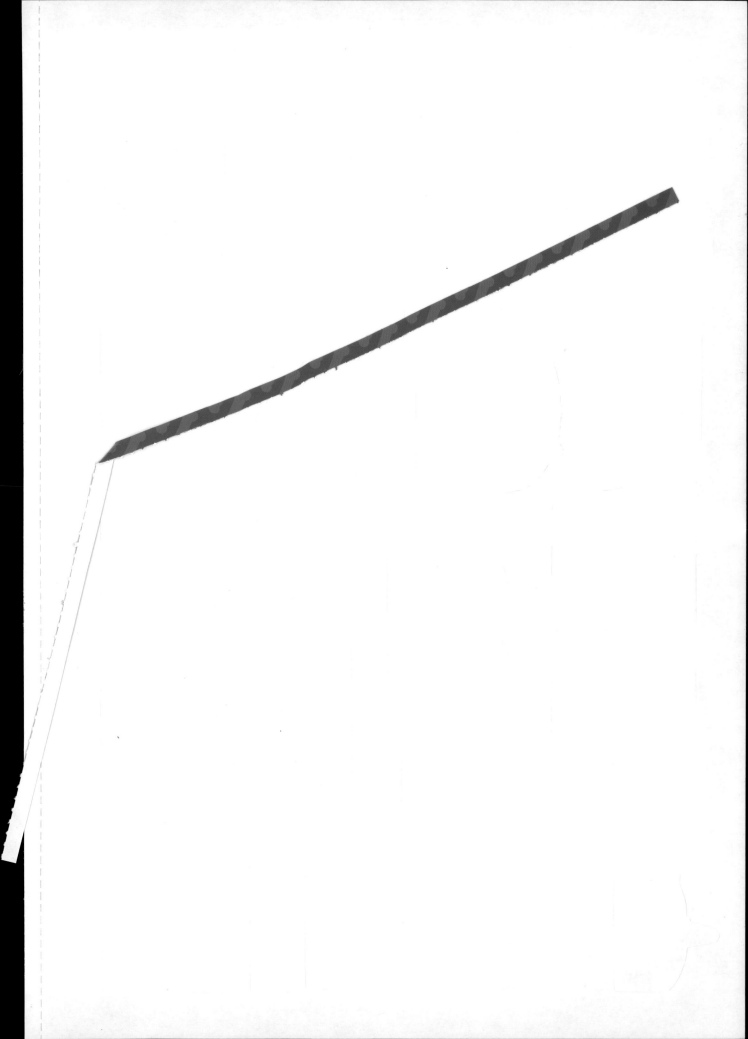

PUZZLE 11

11

2

8

4

5

14

3

16

7

10

15

9

18 19

17

6

1

12

13

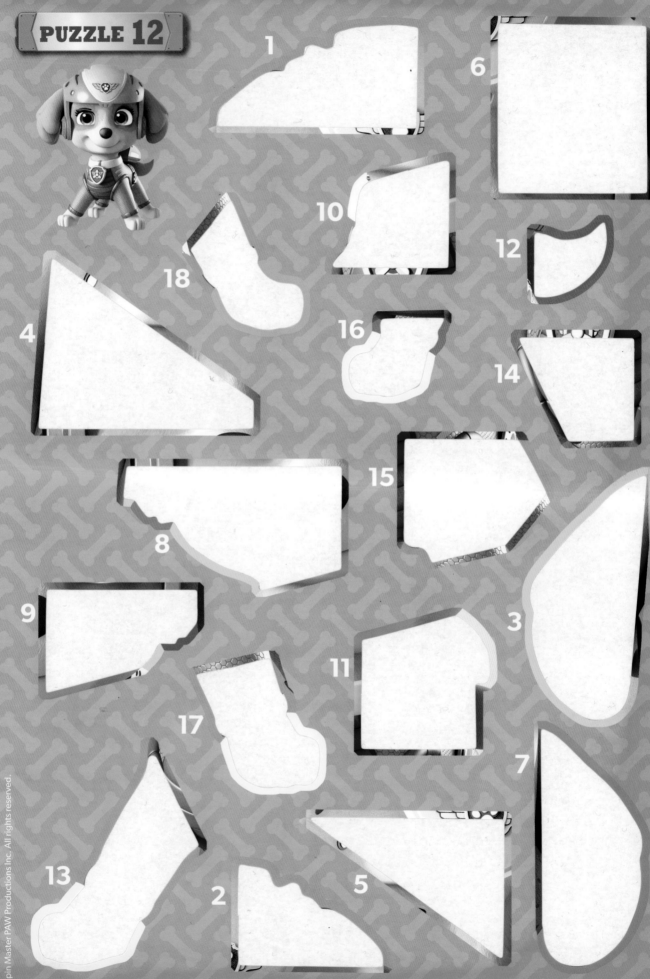

PUZZLE 12

1

6

10

12

18

4

16

14

8

15

9

3

11

17

7

13

2

5

Help Zuma get to his hovercraft.

START

FINISH

Use the key to color this picture.

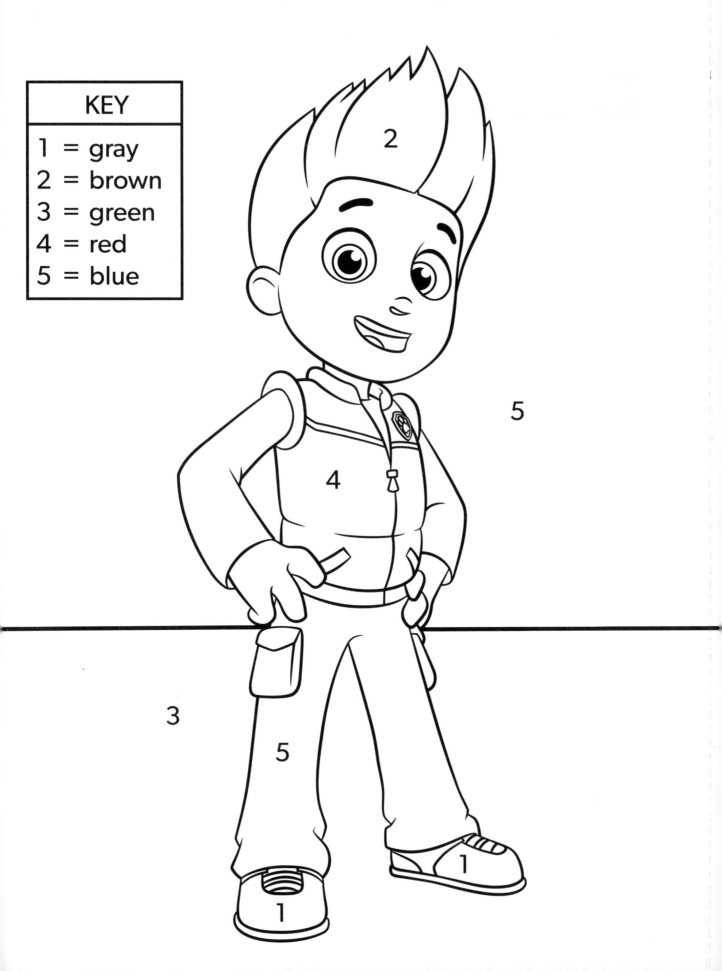

KEY
1 = gray
2 = brown
3 = green
4 = red
5 = blue

PUZZLE 7

Connect the dots to meet Rocky's new friend.

All paws on deck!
Help Marshall and Rocky get to Ryder.

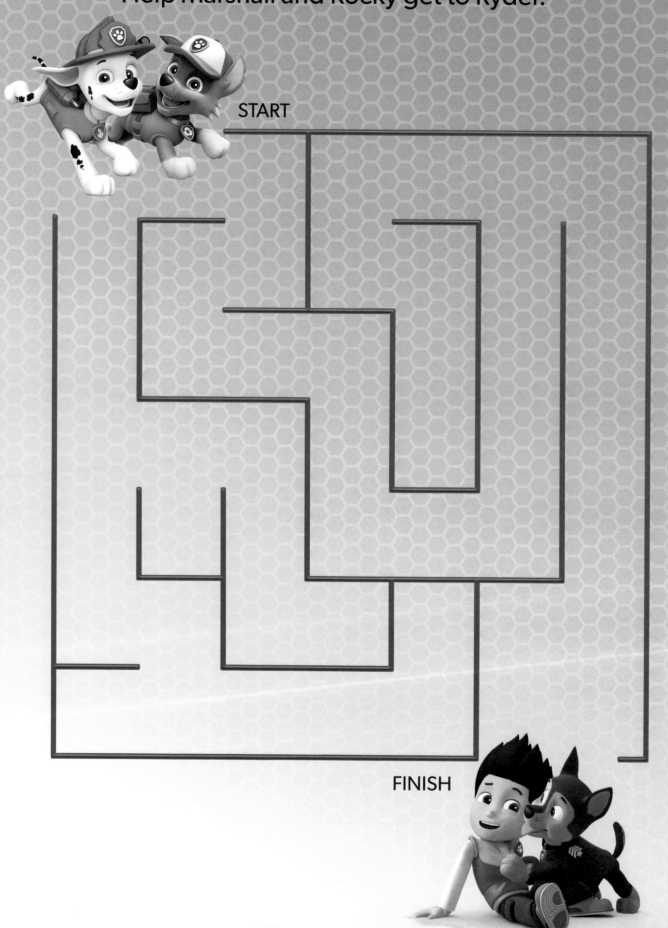

START

FINISH

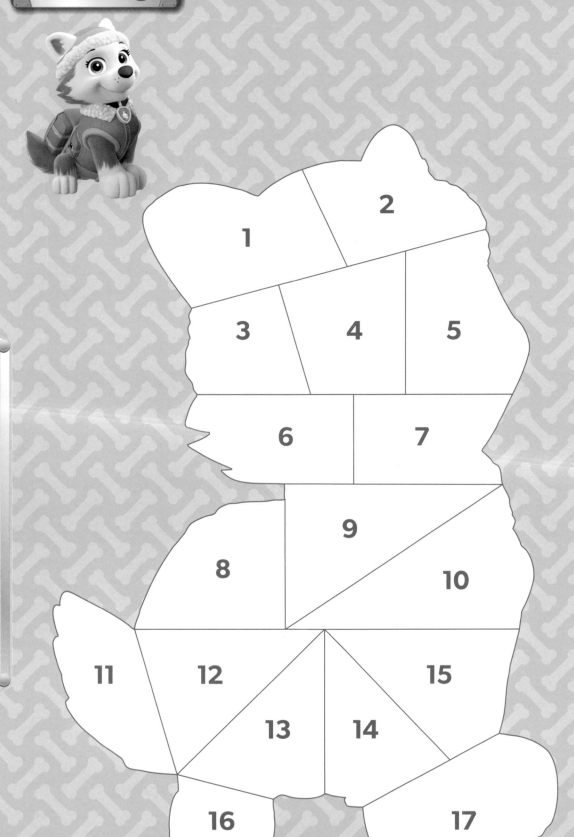

Can you find Everest's snowmobile?
(Hint: It's the one that's different.)

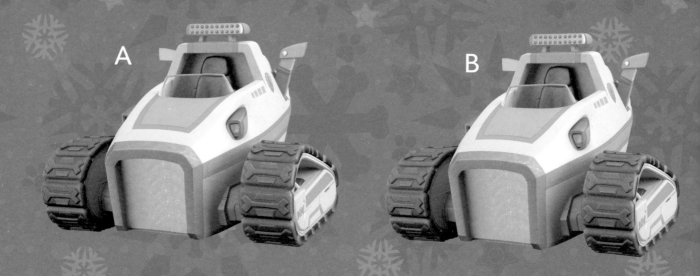

A

B

C

D

E

Help Chase find Tracker. Don't go past the cones!

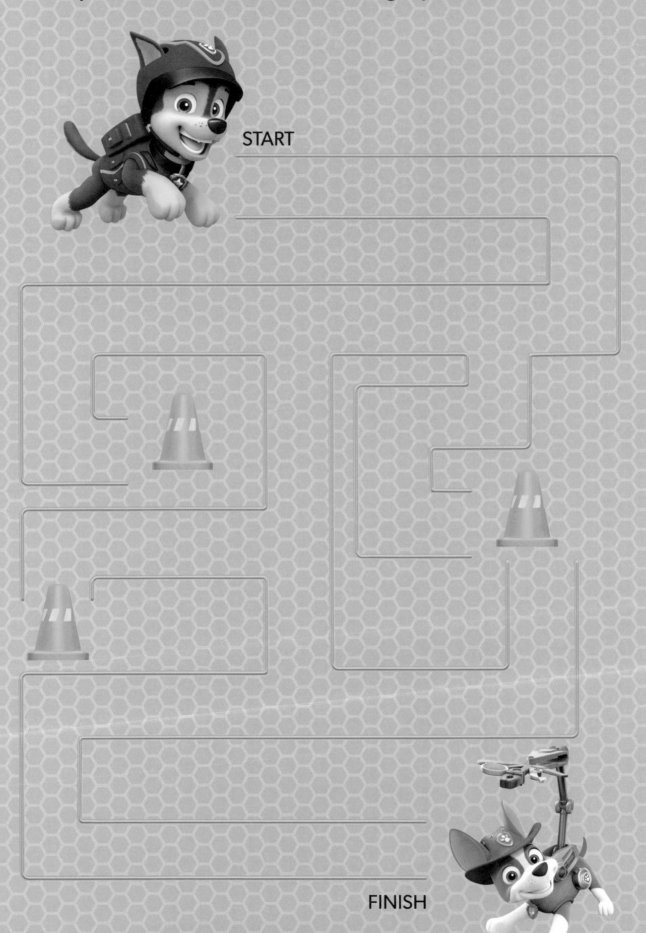

START

FINISH

1

2

3

4

5

6

7

8

9

10

11

12

13

14

15

Match each member of the team to his or her close-up.

A

B

C
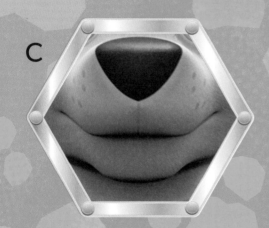

1

2

3

ANSWER: A-2, B-1, and C-3.

Circle the two Air Patrollers that match.

To complete this picture of Rubble, fill in the missing boxes. Use the top picture as a guide.

Use the key to color this picture.

KEY	
1 = red	4 = green
2 = orange	5 = yellow
3 = brown	

1
2
3
5
7
9
4
6
8
10
11
13
12
14
16
19
15
17
18

Match each member of the team to his close-up.

A

B

C

 1

 2

 3

ANSWER: A-3, B-2, and C-1.

Color the bottom picture of Skye so it matches the top picture.